Stephen Hillenburg (signature)

Based on the TV series *SpongeBob SquarePants*® created by Stephen Hillenburg
as seen on Nickelodeon®

SIMON SPOTLIGHT
An imprint of Simon & Schuster Children's Publishing Division
1230 Avenue of the Americas, New York, New York, 10020
Copyright © 2003 Viacom International Inc. All rights reserved.
NICKELODEON, *SpongeBob SquarePants,* and all related titles, logos,
and characters are trademarks of Viacom International Inc.

Manufactured in the United States of America
First Edition
2 4 6 8 10 9 7 5 3 1

ISBN 0-689-85878-7

SpongeBob's Christmas Wish

adapted by Kim Ostrow

based on the teleplay by Mr. Lawrence, Mark O'Hare,
Merriweather Williams, Derek Drymon, and Stephen Hillenburg

illustrated by C.H. Greenblatt and William Reiss

Simon Spotlight/Nickelodeon
New York   London   Toronto   Sydney   Singapore

SpongeBob creeped quietly to the door of Sandy's treedome.

"Haaaaa! I'm gonna get that Sandy with a super-sneaky karate move," said SpongeBob.

He peeked through Sandy's window just as she was about to plug in her Christmas lights.

As soon as the tree lit up, SpongeBob shouted, "Fire! Fire! Don't worry, Sandy, I'm coming!"
With that, he burst through the door and poured a bucket of water on her head.

"What in the name of Alamo is wrong with you, SpongeBob?" she asked.

"I guess there's no fire," he replied sheepishly.

"Haven't you ever seen a Christmas tree?" asked Sandy.

"Christmas who?" SpongeBob asked. "Is she a friend from Texas?"

So Sandy sat down and told SpongeBob all about her favorite holiday. She told him about the toy-making elves and flying reindeer, about baking cookies and hanging stockings, and best of all, she told him about Santa Claus.

SpongeBob ran to the Krusty Krab to tell
his friends about Christmas.

"And everyone pretends to like fruitcake," SpongeBob reported. "But,
the best part is that you can write a letter to this guy, Santa Claus. You
just tell him what you want and he brings it to you."

"I don't know about you lubbers," said Mr. Krabs, "but any feller who
is giving away free stuff is a friend of mine!"

"That's the spirit!" cried SpongeBob. "Here's some paper. You can all get started on your letters."

Squidward rolled his eyes. "I can't believe anybody would celebrate a holiday where a jolly prowler breaks into your house and leaves gifts."

"Come on, Squidward, write a letter,"
begged SpongeBob.
Squidward shook his head. "Grow up, would ya? No one's
going to give me a gift just because I
write him a stupid letter."

Patrick was trying to write his letter, but the paper kept ripping in half. SpongeBob showed him how to do it.

"Dear Santa," SpongeBob wrote as he began his own letter. "What do I want for Christmas you may ask? All I want is for you to visit the gentle folk of Bikini Bottom. That is my wish."

Later that day SpongeBob showed Patrick his invention for sending letters to Santa.

"See, Patrick, you put your letter in the bottle, stick the bottle into the machine, and then . . . fire in the hole!" he shouted as the bottle shot out of Bikini Bottom and up to the surface.

"Neat!" said Patrick. "Send mine!"

"What did you wish for?" asked SpongeBob as he loaded Patrick's bottle.

"Another piece of paper," Patrick said with a sigh.

Soon everyone arrived with their wishes tucked into bottles.
"What did you wish for, little girl?" asked SpongeBob.
"Front teeth," she replied hopefully.

Then Squidward pushed through the crowd.

"What's *your* wish?" SpongeBob asked him.

Squidward scowled. "My wish is that the people of Bikini Bottom will stop paying attention to the ridiculous dribble that is constantly streaming out of this dunderhead's mouth."

"Gee, Squidward," said SpongeBob, smiling, "maybe Santa will bring me a dictionary so I can understand what you just said!"

"Now that we have summoned Santa Claus," SpongeBob announced,
"we must ready ourselves for his arrival."
Everyone cheered.

When SpongeBob realized Squidward had not yet sent a letter, he rushed over to help him. "I am not writing a letter to a figment of your imagination, SpongeBob!" yelled Squidward. SpongeBob opened his eyes very wide. "But, Squidward, when Santa comes you'll be the only one without a gift!"

"How many times do I have to say it? I don't believe in Santa Claus!" Squidward shouted.

That night everyone but Squidward stayed up all night waiting for
Santa to arrive. Morning came . . . but Santa didn't.

"Hey, where's Santa?" asked a little fish.

"Uh . . . he should be here any minute!" said a very tired SpongeBob.

"Thanks for the lies, Mr. Fairy Tale!" said a big fish.
One by one, they all left SpongeBob standing alone.
"Where's your Christmas spirit?" SpongeBob shouted after them.
"He's probably just running late!"
"Yeah, he probably just stopped for a sandwich," said Patrick,
trying to help.

When Squidward woke up that morning, he looked out his window. He didn't see a single sign of Santa Claus.

"Merry Christmas!" said Squidward as he danced around SpongeBob, laughing.

"You were right. This *is* a stupid holiday," cried SpongeBob, sticking his head in the sand. "But I still want you to have this."

SpongeBob handed Squidward a neatly wrapped box.

"I made it for you so you wouldn't feel left out when Santa came," said SpongeBob, his eyes filling up with tears.

"Gee . . . I . . . um . . . I don't know what to say," said Squidward.

"You're welcome," SpongeBob replied. He cried all the way home.

"It's probably a jellyfish net. Or an old Krabby Patty. Or his favorite underpants!" said Squidward as he unwrapped the present.

When he opened the box he found a clarinet made out of driftwood with his name carved into it. Squidward pressed a button and three little Squidwards popped out and played music!

"Wow. I feel horrible! What have I done to poor SpongeBob?"

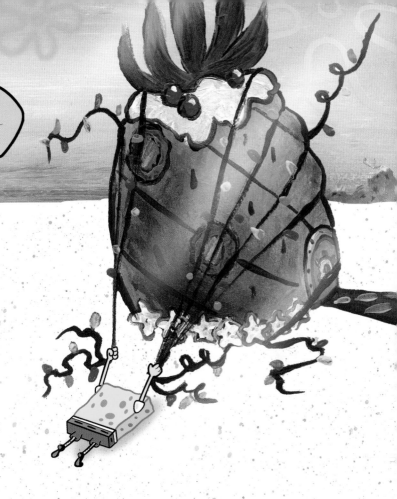

Squidward looked out the window and saw SpongeBob crying as he took down his Christmas lights.

All of a sudden Squidward had a brilliant idea. . . .

"Ho! Ho! Ho!" shouted Squidward from his roof.

"Hello? Who's there? What? Show yourself!" said SpongeBob as he spun around looking for the source of the voice.

"Up here, you dunce . . . I mean . . . Merry Christmas, little boy!" said Squidward.

SpongeBob looked up to the roof and his eyes popped wide open. "Could . . . could it be?" he asked.

"Yes, it is I, Santa Claus! Ho! Ho! Whoops!" said Squidward as he tumbled off the roof and landed flat on his nose!

SpongeBob was so excited that all he could do was run in circles, screaming, "You're SSSSSan . . . SSSSSan . . . S, S, S . . ."

"All right, now, take it easy," said Squidward.

"I knew you'd make it!" cried SpongeBob. "Where's your big belly?"

Squidward had to think. "Uh . . . that's the result of . . . uh . . . undersea pressure on my body!"

"Where are your reindeer?" SpongeBob asked. "And your flying machine?"

Squidward had to think fast again. "Uhhh . . . I loaned them to the Easter Bunny!"

"And what about that nose?" he added, honking Squidward's long nose. "I knew you were supposed to have a big one, but that thing's gigantic!"

"All right!" said Squidward, annoyed. "I'm Santa."

SpongeBob hugged him tight. "This is the greatest gift you could have given me. Thank you for bringing Christmas to Bikini Bottom."

Squidward looked into SpongeBob's big, teary eyes and said, "I didn't bring Christmas to Bikini Bottom. You did."

"I did?" asked SpongeBob in disbelief.

Just then a little girl fish walked up to Squidward. "Do you have a present for me, Santa?" she asked.

"Uh . . . just a second," said Squidward. He looked around his house for something to give her and ran back outside with a wrench.

"Thanks, Santa!" she said, delighted with her gift.

"Huh," said Squidward, shrugging. "That almost felt good."

When Squidward turned around, everyone in Bikini Bottom was lined up on his lawn waiting for a present from Santa. Squidward gave each of them something from his house, and before he realized it, he had given away everything he owned.

"What was I thinking?" he cried. "I gave away all my stuff just so SpongeBob wouldn't be sad. Am I insane?"

Just then there was a knock on Squidward's door.

"You missed him!" shouted SpongeBob as Squidward opened the door. "He came! He gave us all presents! He was jolly and had a beard! He was friendly and kind and Santa-ish! His belly was small, but his nose was *huge* with Christmas joy!"

SpongeBob was talking a mile a minute. Squidward just spun him around and nudged him toward home.

"Well, at least it's over," said Squidward with a sigh.

He looked down and noticed a letter in a bottle on his doorstep. "What's this?" he wondered aloud.

Dear Squidward,
Thanks for all your help. You've been a really good boy this year!
Warm regards,
Santa

Squidward looked up and caught a glimpse of the real Santa Claus, with all of his reindeer, flying overhead.

Squidward blew into his clarinet. "Yup," he said. "I'm insane."